This rising moon book belongs to 2007

A. S. Burris

a book about writing letters to our most darling
of niece's ... love from your favourite Aunties,

Auntie Boo Burris!

and Auntie Jeanne
and Auntie Liz ☺
and Auntie 'Lissa, too!

Thank You, Aunt Tallulah!

by Carmela LaVigna Coyle

Illustrated by Bruce MacPherson

A **rising moon**
PRODUCTION

www.risingmoonbooks.com

Composed in the United States of America
Printed in China

Edited by Theresa Howell
Designed by Katie Jennings

The author would like to thank the British Antarctic Survey.
www.antarctica.ac.uk

FIRST IMPRESSION 2006

ISBN-13: 978-0-87358-891-1
ISBN-10: 0-87358-891-6

06   07   08   09   10   5   4   3   2   1

Library of Congress Cataloging-in-Publication Data

Coyle, Carmela LaVigna.
Thank you, Aunt Tallulah! / by Carmela LaVigna Coyle ;
illustrated by Bruce MacPherson.
p. cm.
Summary: The many mishaps of Bettina, who is attending summer camp,
and her Aunt Tallulah,
who is living at the South Pole, are described in the letters they exchange.
ISBN-13: 978-0-87358-891-1 (hardcover)
ISBN-10: 0-87358-891-6 (hardcover)
[1. Letters—Fiction. 2. Aunts—Fiction. 3. Camps—Fiction. 4. South Pole—Fiction.
5. Humorous stories.]
I. MacPherson, Bruce W., 1960- ill. II. Title.
PZ7.C839478Tha 2006
E]—dc22
2005027584

To lively aunts everywhere—especially my sister,
Auntie Thea (who doesn't look anything like Aunt Tallulah)!
—C.L.V.C.

To Debbie
—B.M.

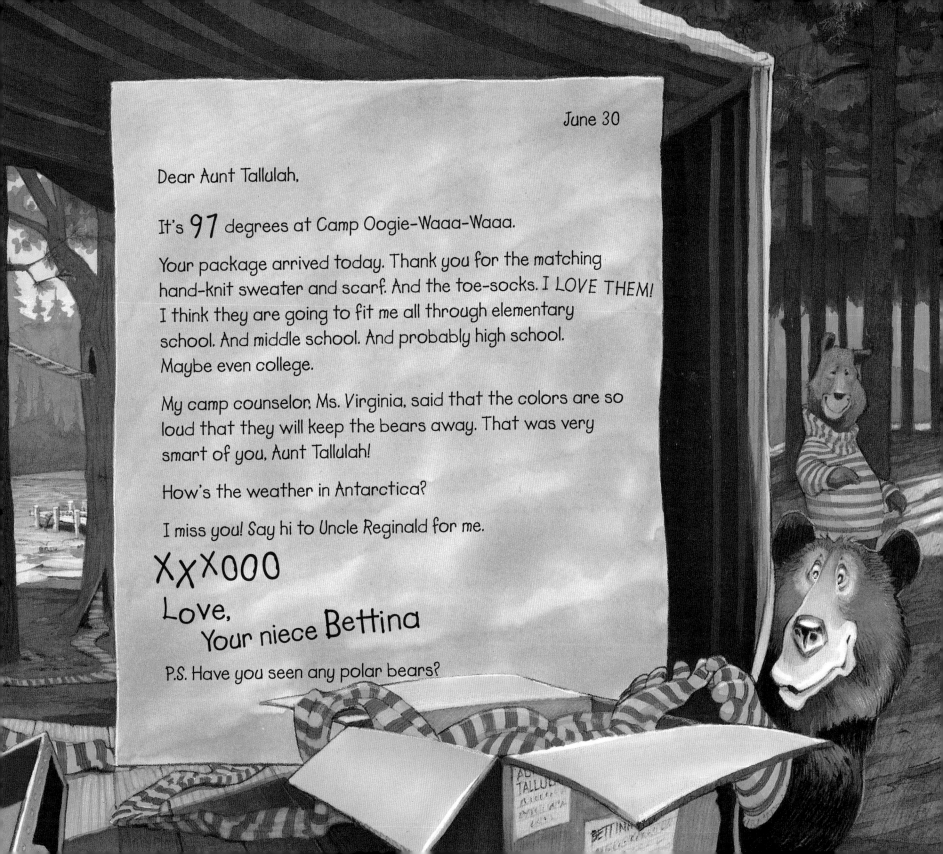

June 30

Dear Aunt Tallulah,

It's **97** degrees at Camp Oogie-Waaa-Waaa.

Your package arrived today. Thank you for the matching hand-knit sweater and scarf. And the toe-socks. I LOVE THEM! I think they are going to fit me all through elementary school. And middle school. And probably high school. Maybe even college.

My camp counselor, Ms. Virginia, said that the colors are so loud that they will keep the bears away. That was very smart of you, Aunt Tallulah!

How's the weather in Antarctica?

I miss you! Say hi to Uncle Reginald for me.

XXXOOO

Love,
    Your niece Bettina

P.S. Have you seen any polar bears?

July 8

Dear Bettina,

It's -40 degrees in Antarctica.

You're most welcome, dear. I am glad you like everything. And thank you for your note. Your handwriting is really quite lovely.

What's new at camp?

As usual, it's dark all night and day during Antarctica's winter months of May, June, and July. Uncle Reginald calls it "sweater weather" because it's when I do all my knitting—which brings me to your sweater. I really can't take credit for the noisy colors. With all this dark, I thought it was blue!

Uncle Reginald sends his love. I've sent you another package!

Love,

Aunt Tallulah

P.S. Interestingly, polar bears do not live at the South Pole, only up at the North Pole.

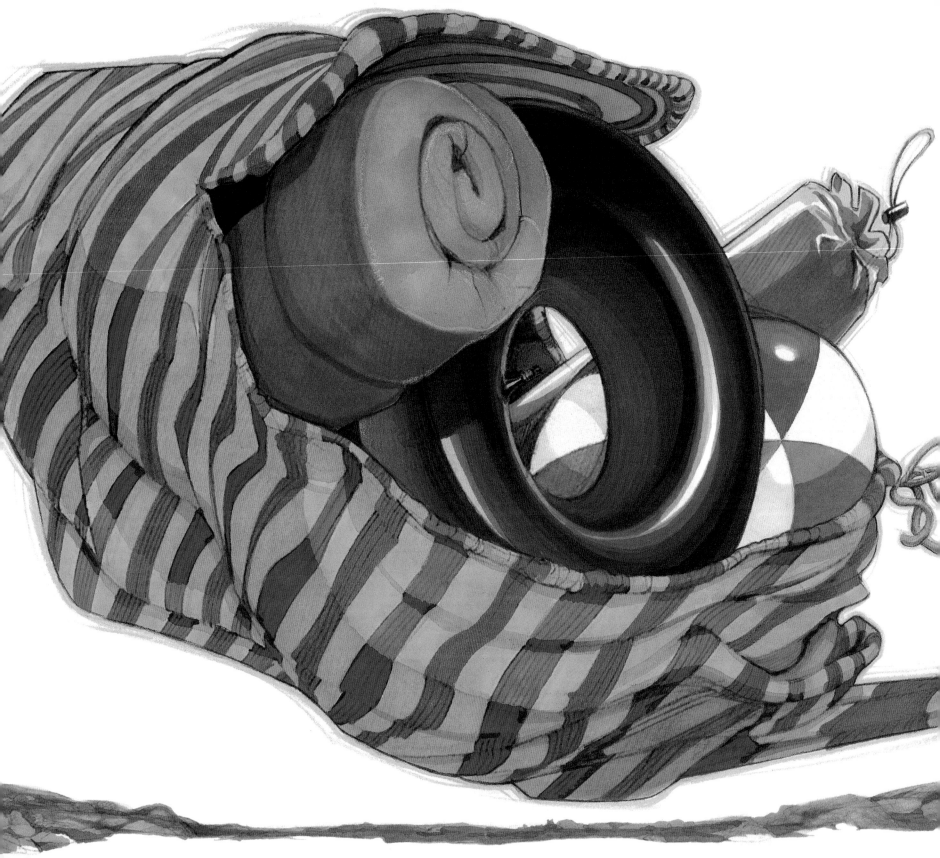

July 16

Dear Aunt Tallulah,

It's 98 degrees at Camp Oogie-Waaa-Waaa.

The second package arrived today. **What a surprise!**
Thanks for the knitted backpack. I can get all of my stuff
inside of it, including my sleeping bag. And pillow. I might
even be able to get my tent in there. The backpack
matches the sweater set so perfectly that maybe
everyone should knit in the dark!

Camp Oogie-Waa-Waa is so much fun!

My very favorite parts are swimming and food.
Today, I swam to the other side of the lake for
a double banana split with sprinkles.

Thank you, Aunt Tallulah!

♡ Bettina

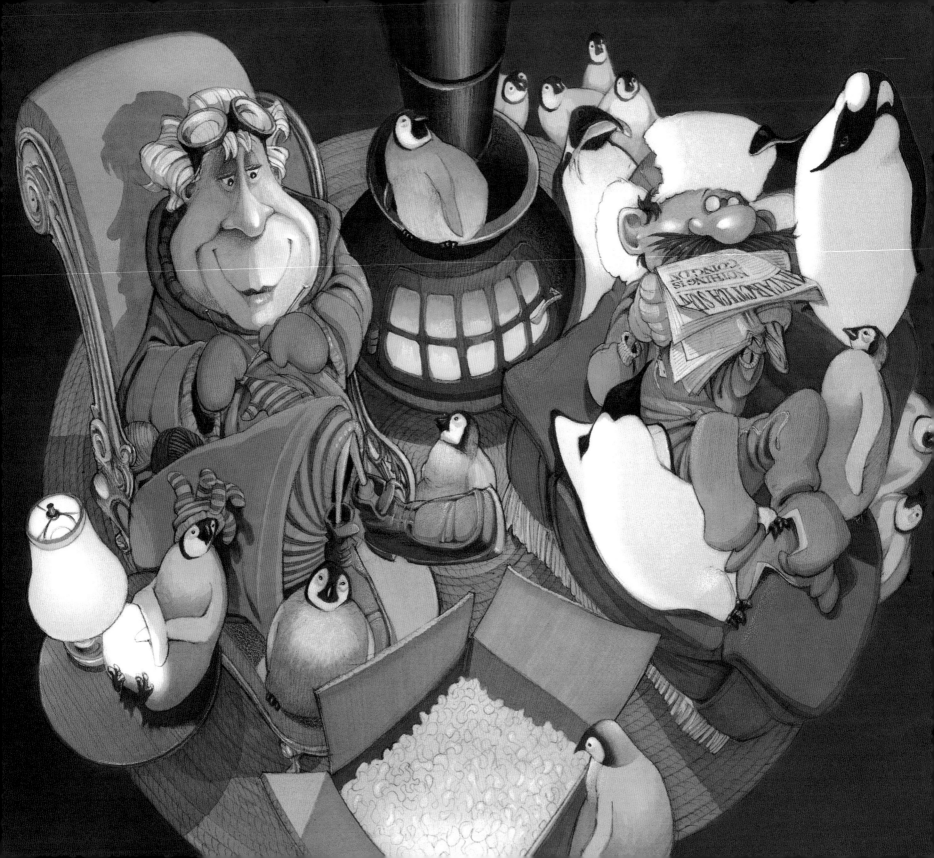

July 26

Dear Bettina,

Thank you for your note, dear. I am happy
that the second package arrived safely.
Although, I must tell you that the "backpack" is a hat!

Brrr. It's -45 degrees today! Yesterday,
your Uncle Reginald got lost in a blizzard
and ended up spending the night in a
penguin rookery. *He's fine*, but now all
the young penguins think he's their papa.
And so do the mamas.

I'm shipping you another small goody
package. I won't give away the surprise.
Be looking for it in the mail.

Love,
Your Aunt Tallulah

August 1

Dear Aunt Tallulah,

It's **99** degrees at Camp Oogie-Waaa-Waaa.

The goody package arrived this afternoon!

Thank you for the gloves. They are really...cool. In fact they were still partly frozen when they arrived. I like how they match my sweater.

And my toe-socks.

And my backpack—I mean, hat.

Was there a reason that you knitted six fingers in the right-hand glove?

Thank you, Aunt Tallulah.

LOVE,
Your niece **Bettina**

P.S. Here is a picture of me by the swimming hole wearing my sweater set and hat. The other people in the picture are my new camp friends.

August 8

Dear Bettina,

It's -31 degrees in Antarctica.

I'm delighted that you received the package
so quickly.

The photograph was lovely. You look stunning
in your outfit. Your new friends at Camp
Boogie-Waaa-Waaa look so happy, especially
the ones pointing at you.

As far as the glove with the sixth finger
goes—Oops! You'll think of some clever use
for it.

Yesterday, Uncle Reginald's mustache froze
to his camera while filming the Southern
Lights. *He's fine*, but no more mustache!

Love,
Your Aunt Tallulah

P.S. I've enclosed a snapshot
of the Southern Lights. Our
sky looks like this every
time solar heat gets trapped
in the higher atmosphere.

Southern Lights

August 14

Dear Aunt Tallulah,

It's 101 degrees at Camp Oogie-Waaa-Waaa.

I will miss Uncle Reginald's mustache. It made him look like he was always smiling.

Thank you for the snapshot and explanation of the pretty lights. I had no idea!

I finally finished my camp craft project this afternoon. I made it out of pipe-cleaners and pinecones. Actually, I had enough time to make two, so I am mailing them to you and Uncle Reginald as a surprise. I hope they fit!

Love,
Your niece Bettina

August 2(

Dear Bettina,

My! What a surprise! Uncle Reginald and
I love your gifts. Thank you, dear.
Your artistry is superb.

I must tell you, though, just seconds
after this photo was taken, Uncle
Reginald fell through the ice!
He's fine, but his eyeglasses aren't.
Luckily your brilliant swimsuit saved
his life! The pinecones acted as
marvelous buoys!

Love,
Aunt Tallulah &
Uncle Reginald

P.S. Enclosed you'll find video footage
of the entire incident.

August 26

Dear Aunt Tallulah,

Wow! What a film! My camp counselor, Ms. Virginia, is going to use it to teach campers water survival techniques. (Although she plans to edit the sound.)

I especially liked the part when Uncle Reginald gets pulled from the icy waters by that walrus.

Love,
Bettina

P.S. Yeah! I'm going home tomorrow!
I sure will miss the banana splits.

September 1

Dear Bettina,

I'm glad your camp counselor found a good use for the film. However, darling, that was not a walrus pulling Uncle Reginald out of the water. It was *me* in a parka.

Good news! We leave next week for the Amazon! Uncle Reginald has been asked to film a documentary on the effect that mail-order catalogs have on monkeys.

Here's our new address:

Dr. and Mrs. Reginald Wilding Ph.D.
River Barge #52
Amazon Valley, Peru
SOUTH AMERICA

Love,

Aunt Tallulah

P.S. I bet it feels good to be home. Perhaps you can visit us in the Amazon sometime!

September 7

Dear Aunt Tallulah,

It does feel good to be home. Sort of...

Yesterday, I gave my parents the pinecone and pipe cleaner
floaties I made for them at camp.

Warning! Pinecone floaties can puncture large inflatable
pools causing whitewater conditions!

I had no idea! Neither did mother and dad.

We would love to come visit you in the Amazon sometime!
Give Uncle Reginald a big hug for me.

Love,
Bettina

P.S. Please send a photo of the Amazon!

He's fine, but...

That's a wrap!

out takes!